JOHN TABOR'S RIDE

by Edward C. Day

illustrated by Dirk Zimmer

Alfred A. Knopf ✦ New York

For Jeff and Alex
E.C.D.

To Brooks-Tabor, Sassy, and Ralph
D.Z.

THIS IS A BORZOI BOOK PUBLISHED BY ALFRED A. KNOPF, INC.
Text copyright © 1989 by Edward C. Day
Illustrations copyright © 1989 by Dirk Zimmer
All rights reserved under International and Pan-American Copyright
Conventions. Published in the United States by Alfred A. Knopf, Inc.,
New York, and simultaneously in Canada by Random House
of Canada Limited, Toronto. Distributed by
Random House, Inc., New York.
Manufactured in Singapore
2 4 6 8 10 9 7 5 3 1

Library of Congress Cataloging-in-Publication Data
Day, Edward C. John Tabor's ride / by Edward C. Day ;
illustrated by Dirk Zimmer.
p. cm.
Summary: John Tabor complains about everything on his first
whaling voyage until he meets a strange old man who takes
him on an extraordinary journey.
[1. Tall tales. 2. Whaling—Fiction. 3. Voyages and travels—Fiction.]
I. Zimmer, Dirk, ill. II. Title.
PZ7.D3297Jo 1989 [E]—dc19 88-9065
ISBN 0-394-88577-5 ISBN 0-394-98577-X (lib. bdg.)

AUTHOR'S NOTE

Nearly one hundred fifty years ago, a whaling ship sailed out of New Bedford, Massachusetts, embarked on a long voyage to the other side of the world. Aboard was a harpooner named John Tabor who had spent twenty years at sea, "a genuine son of Neptune." Like most sailors of the time, Tabor led a hard life and received little reward for his work. He had no home but his ship, and his neighborhood was the always-changing seas. Sailing with him on that voyage was a young college graduate named J. Ross Browne, who had signed on as an ordinary seaman. Browne kept a journal of his adventure and in 1846 published a book, *Etchings of a Whaling Cruise,* telling of his experiences. So authentic was Browne's book that Herman Melville later made use of the account when writing his great novel *Moby Dick.*

One moonlit night in the Indian Ocean, John Tabor related a strange yarn about a mysterious old man he'd met and a fantastic ride on a whale. Browne suggested to the harpooner that it must have been a dream, but Tabor wasn't so sure about that. *John Tabor's Ride* is based on the real John Tabor's yarn.

I discovered John Tabor's tale when the publishing house for which I was working prepared a new reprint edition of *Etchings.* The curious yarn intrigued me because my ancestors had been sailing ship captains and ship-builders, and I had spent three years at sea myself. It seemed to me that my children, and others, might enjoy the story of John Tabor's fantastic ride as much as I did.

n the days when ships were wood and the wind was fuel,
John Tabor set sail on his first great whaling voyage. A brash young
sailor from a family of sailors, he had never been long from home
or worked to earn his keep.

He complained about the food.

He complained about the hard work.

He complained about his uncomfortable bed.

And most of all, he complained about the many months that had to pass before he could go home to Taborstown.

Most whalers accepted their lot, so it wasn't long before the crew grew tired of his constant grumbling.

"John Tabor, ye'd best hush yer fussing, if ye know what's good fer ye," a kindly sailor warned him.

But the young man didn't change his ways.

He complained about the wind.

He complained about the hot sun.

He complained about the smell from boiling down the blubber.

One night John Tabor was wishing he were home instead of on this empty deck, anchored off the coast of Africa, when he heard a voice call out.

"Thar she blows!"

Spinning around, he saw an old man, not more than five feet tall. His beard was covered with tar and hung in strings like rope yarns, and although he must have been more than a hundred years old, he looked as spry and active as a porpoise.

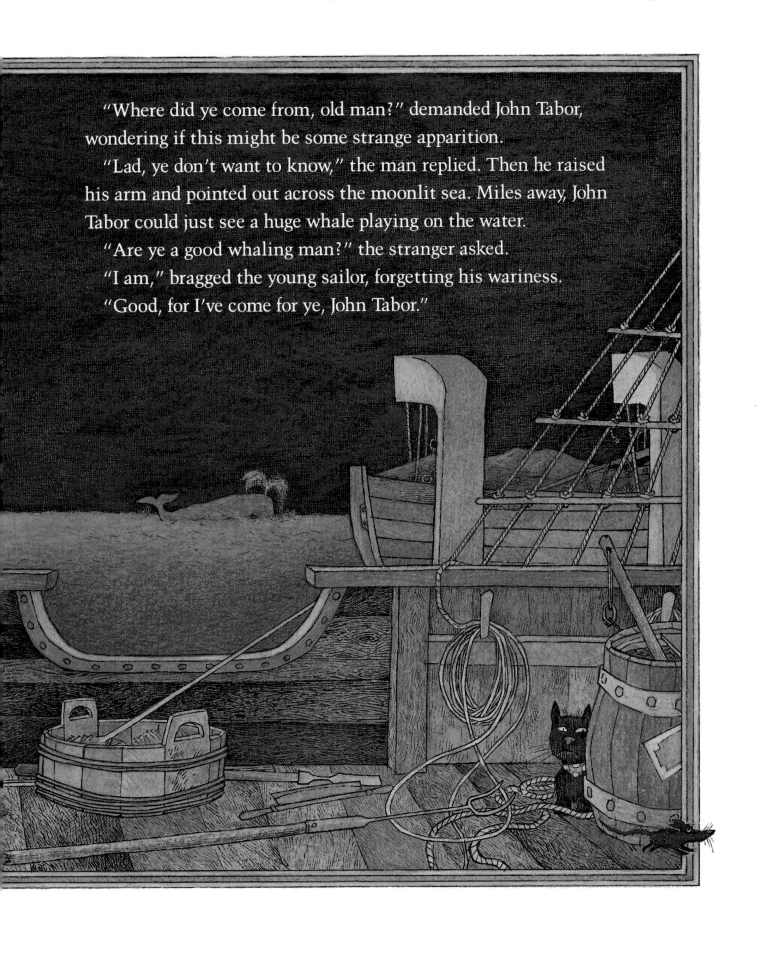

"Where did ye come from, old man?" demanded John Tabor,
wondering if this might be some strange apparition.

"Lad, ye don't want to know," the man replied. Then he raised
his arm and pointed out across the moonlit sea. Miles away, John
Tabor could just see a huge whale playing on the water.

"Are ye a good whaling man?" the stranger asked.

"I am," bragged the young sailor, forgetting his wariness.

"Good, for I've come for ye, John Tabor."

Without further delay the ancient whaler lowered a boat into
the sea and, grasping the sailor by the arm, jumped in.

Old Tar Beard rowed and rowed, until at last they drew near the whale.

"Now for a ride!" cried the man excitedly. "Jump on, John Tabor."

"I will not!" protested the sailor to his unearthly companion. Such an odd thing as riding a-whale-back was not for him.

"Jump on, I say!"

"No, no. 'Tis a fearful thing ye ask," the sailor whined.

"Ye must!" shouted old Tar Beard, and again he seized John Tabor and made a mighty leap. Once settled on the whale's back, he began to hum a very unusual sailor's tune.

Feeling something uncommon and hearing the song, the whale set off with the speed of lightning. The land grew smaller in the distance, and soon they were on the broad and empty sea.

"On, old whale! Stick to me, John Tabor!" shouted the antique sailor.

"But where are we bound? You take me back to the ship!" the young man bellowed.

"Belay yer gabbling and hold on for yer life! Ye fussed about yer ship, so now ye'll go where ye wanted."

"Where away?" asked John Tabor, for he had no more idea of where they were than if he had been dropped on the moon.

"Off the lee bow," said Tar Beard. "That's the Cape of Good Hope."

No one ever rounded that famous cape so fast.

On they dashed, bounding from wave to wave. Just as the sun
came up, the old man sang out, "Land ho!"

The sun had risen only a little when the curious trio shot past the island of Saint Helena, once Napoleon's prison, in the middle of the South Atlantic Ocean. The sea grew rough, but still they flew on like wildfire.

"Land ho!" shouted the stranger again. "Cape Hatteras alee."

The young man knew that that stormy cape was in America.

"Shiver me," he cried. "This whale's bewitched!"

They roared through the water so fast that John Tabor thought
he would lose his slippery perch, and his hair stood bolt upright
from fear.

They passed Nantucket Island in the winking of an eye and

were halfway up Cape Cod when Taborstown, the home of all the Tabors, appeared before them. High and dry they landed, yet onward went that great whale, blowing and pitching and tearing up the beach with his enormous flukes.

"Avast there," said John Tabor. "Look out, or ye'll be foul of the town pump!"

But still they flew, helter-skelter down Main Street, scattering children and women, horses and chickens, on every side.

"Thar she blows!" resounded through the town fore and aft. Retired whaling captains hobbled from their cottages after the

huge creature, armed with harpoons and an array of rusty whaling gear.

The hindmost sang out, "That's young John Tabor! Stop that whale, Captain Tabor!"

And the foremost shouted to those behind, "Throw yer irons!"

A great flurry of harpoons bounced off the whale's tough hide.

All the while, the old man with the long tarry beard kept roaring, "Stick fast, John Tabor! Hang on like fury!"

And hang on he did, not daring to jump off until they fetched up solidly against the town pump.

So great was the shock that the old fellow flew head over heels to the ground, leaving the seat of his trousers in John Tabor's firm grip.

"I'm home!" shouted the young man with glee as he slid from his precarious perch.

"Not so fast, lad," said old Tar Beard. "Ye yammered about home, so now I've taken ye there. But this cruise isn't done."

The little man picked up John Tabor as if he were a feather and, with a mighty jump, leaped back atop the creature.

The whale set out once more, going faster by the second.

John Tabor grasped the old man tightly and cried out, "Please, no more! No more!" But Tar Beard paid no attention.

Now they flew skimming over hills and valleys, towns and villages, until, with a glorious dive, they landed in the Mississippi River.

Down that mighty river they dashed as if possessed by the devil, past steamboats, flatboats, and all manner of small craft. They roared like a hurricane through a fleet of fishing boats.

"Hold fast, John Tabor!" yelled Tar Beard above the wind.

The whale tore on, into the Gulf of Mexico and along the coast of South America, over the Andes Mountains in one gigantic leap, and into the broad Pacific Ocean. Still on, past the South Sea Islands to Australia and into the Indian Ocean, past Christmas Island they went with spray flying, and down the east coast of Africa.

At last, after traveling all the way around the world, they fetched up in the bay where the fantastic journey had first begun.

They ran hard ashore and John Tabor was flung off the whale into the fine white sand. There he fastened himself as firm as the stump of a tree.

In an instant the whale was gone, leaving only a great hole to show where it had been.

John Tabor looked pleadingly at the ancient sailor. "Please, old man. Let me go back to my ship."

His eyes flashing like a thousand lights, Tar Beard growled, "Well then, John Tabor, ye've voyaged home. Let that hold ye until yer ship's casks are full of whale oil, for if ye choose to be a whaling man, then a-whaling ye must go. Promise to leave yer mates in peace and do all ye can to make things better than they be. And don't complain about what cannot be helped."

The old man looked straight into John Tabor's eyes as he finished: "Else I'll be back to oblige ye again."

"On my word, I'll never complain again," swore John Tabor.

With that, Tar Beard crinkled his face in a grin and vanished in a flurry of sand.

t is said that after that ride John Tabor became the most jolly whaler in the fleet. Sailors all along the coast flocked to sign on any ship he was in, for he cheered them up with songs and yarns and sailors' dances.

But it is also whispered among those who go to sea for whales that sometimes, at night, John Tabor will stop whatever he is doing and stare over the rail at the ocean. An odd look will come into his eyes, and a shudder pass through him, as if something fearful were out there waiting.